Katie
the Kitten
Fairy

D0414004

For Kate Granlund, with lots of love

Special thanks to Sue Mongredien

If you purchased this book without a cover, you should be aware that this book is stolen property. It was reported as "unsold and destroyed" to the publisher, and neither the author nor the publisher has received any payment for this "stripped book."

No part of this work may be reproduced, stored in a retrieval system, or transmitted in any form or by any means, electronic, mechanical, photocopying, recording, or otherwise, without written permission of the publisher. For information regarding permission, write to Rainbow Magic Limited c/o HIT Entertainment, 830 South Greenville Avenue, Allen, TX 75002-3320.

ISBN-13: 978-0-545-02816-5
ISBN-10: 0-545-02816-7

Text copyright © 2006 by Rainbow Magic Limited.
Illustrations copyright © 2006 by Georgie Ripper.

All rights reserved. Published by Scholastic Inc., 557 Broadway, New York, NY 10012, by arrangement with Rainbow Magic Limited.

SCHOLASTIC, LITTLE APPLE, and associated logos are trademarks and/or registered trademarks of Scholastic Inc. RAINBOW MAGIC is a trademark of Rainbow Magic Limited. Reg. U.S. Patent & Trademark Office and other countries. HIT and the HIT logo are trademarks of HIT Entertainment Limited.

12 11   11 12 13 14/0

Printed in the U.S.A.   40

First Scholastic printing, March 2008

Katie the Kitten Fairy

by Daisy Meadows

LITTLE APPLE

SCHOLASTIC INC.

New York   Toronto   London   Auckland
Sydney   Mexico City   New Delhi   Hong Kong

The Fairyland Palace

Wetherbury Village

Strawberry Farm

The Spring Show

Jack Frost's
Ice Castle

Bramble
Stables

Jane Dillon's House

The Park

Kirsty's
House

Jamie
Cooper's
House

The
Wainwrights'
House

Fairies with their pets I see
and yet no pet has chosen me!
So I will get some of my own
to share my perfect frosty home.

This spell I cast, its aim is clear:
To bring the magic pets straight here.
The Pet Fairies soon will see
their seven pets living with me!

Contents

A Very Unusual Kitten

"Catch!"

Kirsty Tate tossed a baseball into the air. She watched as her friend Rachel Walker ran across the grass to catch it. It was the first day of spring vacation, and Rachel had come to stay with Kirsty's family for a whole week. The two girls were playing in the park while Kirsty's parents were out at the grocery store. The sun was shining brightly, and there wasn't a cloud in the sky. It felt like perfect spring weather.

Rachel held up the ball triumphantly. "Your turn," she called. "Ready?"

Before Kirsty could reply, loud barking rang through the air. Both girls spun around to see a large black dog bounding past them.

Rachel jumped back
as the dog raced by.
"Is that a squirrel it's
chasing?" she asked,
watching the dog
run off.

Kirsty shielded her
eyes from the sun to take a better
look. "No, it's a kitten!" she exclaimed.
Her eyes widened at the sight of a tiny
white-and-gray kitten scrambling across
the grass. "What's a kitten doing in the
park?"

"I don't know — but that
dog's about to
catch it," Rachel
said in alarm.
"Come on!"
The two girls started

to run after the animals. But they hadn't gotten very far before a sudden flash of bright light flickered through the air. A cloud of amber-colored sparkles swirled around the kitten. Seconds later, the kitten had vanished — and an enormous striped tiger had appeared in its place! The tiger turned toward the dog and roared.

Right away, the dog stopped short and put its ears back. Then, with a frightened whimper, it turned and bolted away as quickly as it could.

Kirsty and Rachel watched in disbelief as the tiger turned back into a kitten with another flash of bright sparkles. Then the kitten shook itself off, licked one paw, and padded off happily through the grass.

Rachel rubbed her eyes. "Did you just see that?" she asked, her eyes still fixed on the kitten.

Kirsty nodded. "That looked like fairy magic!" she exclaimed.

Rachel grinned. "That's exactly what I thought," she replied. Whenever she and Kirsty were together, they always had the best magical adventures. This looked like it might be the start of another one!

Rachel paused thoughtfully. "But . . . we haven't seen any fairies here!"

Kirsty frowned. "That is strange, isn't it?" she said. "Let's follow the kitten. Maybe it will lead us to a fairy!"

The two girls hurried after the small kitten. It didn't seem to be in any real rush as it wandered along, stopping to pounce on a daisy or bat at a blade of grass.

"Where do you think it's going?"
Rachel whispered. "It seems like it's
heading right for the fence."

They both watched as the kitten
walked cheerfully toward a wooden
fence at the edge of the grass. The fence
was too high for the kitten to climb over,
but it showed no sign of changing
direction.

"How is the kitten going to —" Kirsty
started. Then she broke off
in surprise.

With another swirl of
sparkles, the kitten
had suddenly
shrunk! Now it
was the size of a
mouse, small enough
to squeeze through a

tiny hole at the bottom of the fence.
Kirsty's eyes widened as she watched its
little gray tail disappear through the hole.

"Wow!" Rachel gasped, staring after
the kitten. "Quick — there's a gate in the
fence over that way. We can't lose
track of that kitten!"

Both girls rushed
through the gate,
and saw that the
kitten was full-size
again. The only
sign that it had
ever been any
different was a
faint trail of
magical sparkles
glimmering
behind it.

Just then, the kitten twitched its whiskers and bounded toward a fast food cart. As the girls got closer, they saw it run up to a man who was standing by the vendor.

"Fish sticks and fries, please," the girls heard him say.

The kitten meowed loudly. It wound itself between the man's legs as the vendor handed him a plateful of food.

The man chuckled. "Sorry, kitty," he said, sitting down on a nearby bench. "This is my lunch, not yours."

As the man began to eat, Kirsty elbowed Rachel and nodded toward the kitten. Its eyes were glowing a bright green. A small cloud of amber-colored sparkles glittered in the air as the kitten looked up hopefully at the man's food. A second later, a fish stick tumbled off the man's plate and landed at the kitten's feet!

With a happy meow, the kitten
pounced on the fish stick
and began to
eat it.

The man
laughed. "It's
your lucky
day, kitty," he
said. "How did I
knock that off the plate?"

Rachel and Kirsty grinned at each
other. They knew that the sneaky kitten
had used magic to make the fish stick fall
to the ground.

"That was definitely fairy magic!"
Kirsty exclaimed. She watched as the
kitten gobbled up the fish stick, cleaned
its whiskers, and trotted off down a
tree-lined path.

"Yes," Rachel agreed. "Something strange is going on! Let's see where the kitten goes now." The girls set off after the kitten again.

They hadn't gotten far when they heard a scuffling sound along the side of the path. Suddenly, six green goblins jumped out from behind a tree! They were all clutching butterfly nets.

"There it is!" shouted one of the goblins, pointing at the kitten. "Get it!"

Surprise Attack!

"Goblins!" Kirsty cried in surprise.
"Oh, no!"

At the sight of the goblins, the kitten's
fur stood on end and its tail fluffed up like
a prickly brush. It hissed at the goblins,
then turned and ran away from them,
toward the girls. With nowhere else to
go, it leaped right up into Rachel's arms!

"Oh!" Rachel gasped, surprised to find the little bundle of fur in her arms. She held the kitten to her body protectively as the goblins approached.

"Give us that kitten!" one of them ordered. "It belongs to Jack Frost, and we've been sent here to bring it home," he added.

Kirsty and Rachel hesitated. They'd met Jack Frost's goblins many times before, and knew what sneaky creatures they could be. Could they really trust the goblins to be telling the truth?

The kitten gave a soft meow, and both girls looked down at it. Its eyes were shining bright green again. Sparkles streamed out of its mouth and swirled around in the air! The kitten meowed again, but this time the girls could hear words in its meows.

"Don't believe those terrible goblins," the kitten declared. "I belong to Katie the Kitten Fairy, but I'm lost!"

Kirsty's fingers quickly closed over the locket around her neck. She and Rachel had been given matching gold lockets full of fairy dust by the fairy king and queen. The fairy dust would take them straight to Fairyland if they ever needed help. Now seemed like a very good time to use the lockets!

"We don't believe you," Rachel told the goblins. "And you're not getting this kitten!" Just then, Kirsty threw golden

fairy dust all over herself, Rachel, and the kitten.

With angry cries, two of the goblins dropped their butterfly nets and dove toward the girls. They stretched their gnarled green hands out to grab the kitten.

Rachel yelped and tried to dodge out of the way, but luckily, the fairy dust was

already working its magic. The girls were swept up into the sky. Below them, the goblins pounced on empty air and fell onto the grass.

Rachel and Kirsty laughed in relief as they felt the fairy dust whisking them through the air. After a moment, they couldn't see the park below, just a blur of bright, sparkling colors all around them. Rachel held the kitten close, in case it was frightened. It seemed used to fairy magic, though, and snuggled up happily in Rachel's arms. Its little ears blew back in the warm, sparkly breeze.

Moments later, the girls floated softly down to the ground. As the magical breeze died away, they both smiled to see that they were back in Fairyland.

"We're fairies!" Rachel exclaimed happily, fluttering her delicate wings.

"And there's the fairy palace, and the king and queen!" Kirsty cheered, waving as King Oberon and Queen Titania approached. Then she frowned. "They don't look very happy, though."

Rachel watched as the king and queen came closer, followed by a crowd of anxious-looking fairies. Her excitement at being back in Fairyland disappeared as she saw how unhappy they all looked. What was wrong?

Missing Pets!

"Hello, Your Majesties," Rachel said politely, giving the king and queen a curtsy with the kitten still in her arms. "Is everything all right?"

A fairy in a pale yellow dress with long, dark hair suddenly caught sight of the kitten. A happy smile lit up her face.

"You've brought Shimmer back!" she cried. "Oh, thank you, thank you!"

The kitten jumped out of Rachel's arms and scampered over to the pretty fairy. The fairy scooped her up, burying her face in Shimmer's soft, silky fur. "Thank you so much," she said again, putting Shimmer down and turning to hug Kirsty and Rachel. "I'm Katie the Kitten Fairy, and I can't tell you how glad I am to see Shimmer back in Fairyland!"

"You're welcome," Rachel said, smiling.

The king and queen stepped forward. "How nice to see you again, girls," the king said warmly. "These are our Pet Fairies. You've already met Katie. This is Bella the Bunny Fairy, Georgia the Guinea Pig Fairy, Lauren the Puppy Fairy, Harriet the Hamster Fairy, Molly the Goldfish Fairy, and Penny the Pony Fairy."

Each fairy stepped forward when her name was called and curtsied to the girls with a little smile. Kirsty couldn't help noticing that their smiles looked a bit sad.

"So where are all the other pets?" she asked curiously.

The fairies all sighed. "Jack Frost stole them," Queen Titania told the girls sadly. "He took them to his ice castle, and then sent out a ransom note. It said that if the Pet Fairies couldn't find him a pet of his own, he would keep all their magic pets for himself!"

"Oh, no!" Kirsty cried out. "He can't do that!"

"He already has," the king responded. "And without their magic pets, the Pet Fairies can't look after all the pets in your world."

"The Pet Fairies are responsible for helping pets that are lost or homeless," the queen explained. "But they can't do that if their own magic pets are missing."

"Can't we give Jack Frost another pet, so that he'll let the magic pets go?" Rachel suggested.

The queen shook her head. "I'm afraid it's not that simple." She sighed. "In Fairyland, pets *choose* their owners. And no pet has ever chosen Jack Frost."

"I'm not surprised!" Kirsty blurted out. Jack Frost was always causing trouble in Fairyland. No wonder none of the magic pets wanted to live with him!

The king was gazing at Shimmer with a thoughtful expression on his face. "Kirsty, Rachel, where did you find Shimmer?" he asked. "We thought all the magic pets were locked in Jack Frost's ice castle." "She was wandering around in the local park," Kirsty replied. "She looked lost!'

The kitten gave a sudden loud meow, as if she was joining in the conversation.

Katie listened hard, then nodded.

"Shimmer says that all the magic pets
were being kept in Jack Frost's castle,"
she said. "But they managed to escape,
and now they're all roaming around in
the human
world."
  The Pet Fairies
looked very
happy to hear
this, but Shimmer
was still meowing.
Katie listened
again, then bit her
lip. "Jack Frost has
sent out a group
of goblins to catch
them and take them
back to the ice castle," she

announced anxiously. "Oh, our poor little pets!"

The other Pet Fairies gasped, and the king and queen looked worried, too.

"We have to find the pets before the

goblins do!" the queen said, sounding
determined.

Kirsty and Rachel looked at each
other. Then, at the same time, they said,
"We'll help!"

Girls on Guard

All the fairies cheered when the girls
agreed to help.

"Thank you!" King Oberon said,
smiling. "It's very kind of you to help us
again."

"The magic pets may be hard to find,"
Queen Titania warned them. "In
Fairyland, they are tiny, fairy-size pets,

but in the human world, they can be any size they wish. They can also work some fairy magic of their own, so you will have to look very carefully."

Shimmer meowed suddenly and Katie bent her head to listen. Her face turned serious. "Shimmer said that a kitten in the human world needs our help," she told the others. "It has no home. Shimmer and I need to find one for it!" Katie turned to the king and queen. "Can we go rescue the kitten?" The king and queen both hesitated. "We'd love for you to help . . ." the queen began slowly.

"But we don't want the goblins to catch Shimmer," the king finished.

"Maybe we could go with Katie and Shimmer," Kirsty suggested. "We could protect them from the goblins!"

The king and queen looked at each other. Then Queen Titania nodded. "That would be all right," she said. "That's very nice of you girls. But you must all be careful. You know how tricky and mean the goblins can be."

"We'll be careful," Katie said, her face lighting up. "Let's go!" She waved her wand, and a trail of amber-colored fairy dust trailed from it. The dust trickled

down around Kirsty and Rachel, and
suddenly Fairyland blurred before their
eyes. A magical wind swept them up,
and they flew through the air with
Katie and Shimmer.

In a rush of color and light, the girls
found themselves back in their own
world. They were human-size again!

"We're back in the park," Rachel said, looking around. "Watch out for goblins, everyone!"

Katie was still holding tiny Shimmer. She flew to hide on Kirsty's shoulder while the girls looked around for goblins.

Then the magic kitten jumped down from Katie's arms and curled up on Kirsty's shoulder. Kirsty could feel his little tail twitching back and forth.

"That tickles!" she giggled as Shimmer batted playfully at her hair.

"The coast is clear," Rachel said, after the girls had scanned the park. "Let's start looking for a homeless kitten."

"We'll have to search carefully," Katie advised. "If it's scared, it could have hidden somewhere."

The four of them set off, keeping their ears open for meows. Katie flew between the girls at shoulder height, while Shimmer padded along beside her in midair. *It's so much fun to watch him,* Kirsty thought. Even though the

40

tiny kitten was hovering magically in the air, he moved just as if he were on the ground. Sometimes he padded along, occasionally he pounced, and every so often he stopped to stalk a floating dandelion seed, or to chase his own fluffy tail. He seemed particularly interested in the elastic holding Rachel's ponytail, which had a couple of pink stars dangling from it. A few times, he leaped up to catch the stars between his tiny paws.

"Come on, Shimmer, we've got work to do," Katie reminded him. She fluttered over to scoop him out of Rachel's hair.

"Where could that lost kitten be?"

Suddenly, Shimmer pricked up his ears and stopped. His little pink nose turned up and his whiskers twitched as he sniffed the air. Then he took a flying leap down to the ground. In a bright burst of sparkles, he grew to the size of a normal kitten! Shimmer raced off ahead of the girls toward the playground.

"I think he found the kitten!" Katie smiled, flying behind her pet. "Come on, girls!"

Rachel and Kirsty ran after Shimmer as he bolted through the grass. Just before he reached the playground, he swerved toward a tall elm tree and sat at the bottom, looking up at it.

Kirsty, Rachel, and Katie gazed up to see what Shimmer had found. On one of the highest branches, huddled against the trunk and looking down at them with big golden eyes, sat a tiny tabby kitten.

Shimmer's Plan

"Poor little thing!" Kirsty exclaimed.
"It's only a baby!"

Just then, a breeze blew through the
tree, and the tabby kitten pounced on
a leaf that was flapping nearby. It
almost lost its balance and tumbled out
of the tree!

"Careful, kitty," Katie called up. The kitten sat down and started washing its paws.

Shimmer ran a little way up the tree toward the tabby kitten and started meowing. The kitten meowed back eagerly.

"Oh, the poor kitten climbed the tree to get out of the wind last night, and now it's stuck!" Katie translated Shimmer and the other kitten's meows. "It's too scared to climb back down."

"Should I climb up and get it?" Rachel offered.

Before Katie could reply, Shimmer started meowing again. The fairy listened, then looked over at the nearby playground. "Good idea, Shimmer," she said, smiling. Then she turned back to the girls. "Thanks for the offer, Rachel, but Shimmer has someone else in mind for the job," she explained with a grin. She pointed her wand in the direction of the playground. "See that boy in the red shirt at the top of the jungle gym?" she asked.

"The one with black hair?" Kirsty said, squinting.

Katie nodded. "That's the one," she replied. "Would you ask him if he can help you get the kitten down from the tree?"

"OK," Kirsty agreed, confused.

"Trust me," Katie said. "It's very important that it is that boy who rescues this kitten."

She winked at the girls. Shimmer meowed loudly, as if he was agreeing with Katie.

"All right." Rachel laughed. "Come on, Kirsty!"

Shimmer shrank back down to fairy pet size. He and Katie hid in the tree while Rachel and Kirsty ran over to the playground. The dark-haired boy had just jumped off the jungle gym when the girls arrived.

"Hello," Kirsty said, giving him a friendly smile. "I'm Kirsty, and this is Rachel. Could you help us rescue a kitten? It's stuck in a tree."

"We saw how good you are at climbing," Rachel explained. "We were wondering if you could climb up the tree and get it down?"

"Sure," the boy replied eagerly. "My name is James, and I love cats. Where's the kitten?"

The girls pointed out the elm tree. James yelled over to tell his dad where he was going. Then he followed Kirsty and Rachel to the tree.

James looked up at the kitten.
"Don't worry, little kitten!
I'll have you down in
two minutes," he
called, and began
to climb.

Kirsty and
Rachel watched as
he clambered higher
and higher. Just as
he was about to
reach the
branch that the
tabby kitten was
perched on, the kitten
jumped down onto
James's shoulder
and butted its head
gently against the boy's cheek.

Kirsty blinked. It looked like a haze of amber-colored sparkles surrounded James and the kitten. She glanced at Rachel and they both grinned knowingly — more Pet Fairy magic!

James carefully carried the tabby kitten all the way back down to the ground. "It's so tiny," he marveled, stroking the kitten gently. "I wonder where it lives."

"He doesn't have a collar or a name tag," Kirsty said. "It looks like a stray."

"Here comes my dad," James said as a tall, dark-haired man strolled over. "Dad, look! We found a lost kitten!"

His eyes brightened suddenly. "Hey, Dad — can we keep it?"

James's dad smiled. "Your mom and I have been talking about getting you a pet," he said. "But we can't just take this one without checking to make sure it doesn't belong to someone else." He looked around to see if the kitten's owner was somewhere in the park.

"We've been here for a while," Kirsty said politely. "Nobody seems to be looking for the kitten."

"Please?" James asked quickly, as soon as his dad hesitated. "We can take it home with us, and call the animal shelter from our house." He stroked it again. "Oh, it's purring, Dad. It likes me!"

James's dad ruffled his son's hair. "OK, then," he said. "If nobody's reported the kitten missing, then I think you can keep it."

"Hooray!" cheered James, beaming from ear to ear. He tickled the tabby kitten under its chin, and the kitten purred even louder. "Do you think Dusty would be a good name?" James wondered out loud.

Rachel nudged Kirsty. She had spotted a few more flecks of fairy dust twinkling in the air around James and the kitten! "Oh, Dusty would be a wonderful name," she said, trying not to giggle.

"Well, then, Dusty," James's dad said, petting the kitten, "we'd better take you home!"

Grasping Goblins

The girls watched as James and his dad walked away happily with their new kitten.

"Good work, girls!" Katie exclaimed as she came out from her hiding place in the tree. "I think Dusty and James will be very happy together."

Shimmer scampered along a tree branch,

purring loudly to show that he agreed, and the girls laughed.

"Fairy magic is wonderful!" Rachel said with a smile. She watched as Shimmer sniffed at a beetle on a nearby leaf and gave a tiny, fairy-size sneeze. Just then, Kirsty heard a rustling sound from a little higher up in the tree.

She looked up to see a goblin — and then another — and then another! She gasped. There was a whole chain of grinning goblins hanging down from one branch of the tree! The lowest goblin was dangling just above the branch where

Shimmer was perched. He was reaching
out to grab the magic kitten!

"No, you don't!" cried Kirsty, scooping
up Shimmer just in time.

"Give it to me!" the goblin growled,
lunging after the kitten.

Shimmer meowed in alarm as the goblin's fingers came within a whisker of him. But the goblin had reached too far, and the other goblins couldn't hold on to him. They all tumbled to the ground, landing in a big green heap of tangled arms and legs!

"Ouch! You're squishing me!"
grumbled one goblin.

"Get off!" groaned another.

Katie grinned at the girls. "Come on!
Let's go while we have the chance,"
she said.

Kirsty held out her hands and let
Shimmer run through the air to
Katie as they walked
away from the
pile of grumpy
goblins. "I don't
think Jack Frost
will be very
happy when they
come back empty-
handed," Kirsty said,
glancing back over her shoulder.
The goblins were still bickering!

"No, Jack Frost won't be happy," Katie agreed. She suddenly shivered. "He'll send them out again to look for another fairy pet!" She cuddled her kitten tightly at the thought of it. "Let's get you safely back to Fairyland, Shimmer," she said in her sweet voice.

"Good-bye, girls — and thank you for everything." Katie hugged the girls in turn, and then Shimmer nuzzled his tiny nose against each of their faces.

"Good-bye, little Shimmer," Kirsty said, giggling as his fur tickled her nose. "It's been nice to meet you."

"Tell the other Pet Fairies that
we'll keep looking for their
lost pets," Rachel added,
blowing Katie and
Shimmer a kiss.

"We will,"
Katie promised.
"Good-bye!" She
tucked Shimmer
carefully under
one arm, then
waved her wand.
A shower of
amber-colored
lights twinkled
around Katie and

Shimmer, and then they were gone.

Rachel and Kirsty smiled at each other
and headed for home. After all the

excitement, they were both hungry! "I'm
so glad we found a nice home for
Dusty," Rachel said happily.

"Everything worked out perfectly. It couldn't have gone better!"

Kirsty slipped her arm through Rachel's as they walked out of the park gate. "I can't wait to find another one of the lost fairy pets," she said excitedly. "It looks like another fairy adventure isn't far away!"

RAINBOW magic™

THE PET FAIRIES

Katie the Kitten Fairy found her kitten,
Shimmer. Now Rachel and Kirsty
must help

Bella the Bunny Fairy!

Easter Bunny

"Isn't it a perfect day for a party?"
Kirsty Tate said, looking up at the
sapphire-blue sky.

Her best friend, Rachel Walker,
nodded and handed Kirsty a chocolate
egg. Rachel was staying with Kirsty for
spring vacation, and the girls were hiding
Easter eggs. They were getting ready to

throw an Easter party for Jane, Mr. and
Mrs. Dillon's five-year-old daughter.
The Dillons lived down the street from
Kirsty.

"There are some great hiding places
here," Rachel said. She gazed around the
beautiful yard with its green grass and
colorful flowerbeds. She knelt down
and hid the egg under a shrub. "Jane and
her friends will love the Easter egg hunt!"

"It'll be fun," Kirsty agreed, hiding an
egg behind the birdbath.

"How many kids are invited to the
party?" Rachel asked.

"Eleven!" Kirsty replied, her eyes
twinkling. "Mr. and Mrs. Dillon are so
glad that we're helping out! They've
been friends with my mom and dad for a

long time, and Jane is really sweet."
Then she lowered her voice. "Do you
think we'll find another one of the
missing fairy pets today, Rachel?"

"I hope so," Rachel whispered back.
"Let's keep our eyes open!"

RAINBOW magic™

THE RAINBOW FAIRIES

Find the magic in every book!

HIT and the HIT Entertainment logo are
trademarks of HIT Entertainment Limited.
© 2009 Rainbow Magic Limited.
SCHOLASTIC and associated logos are trademarks
and/or registered trademarks of Scholastic Inc.

■ SCHOLASTIC

www.scholastic.com

www.rainbowmagiconline.com

HIT entertainment

RAINBOW

RAINBOW magic™

There's Magic in Every Series!

The Rainbow Fairies

The Weather Fairies

The Jewel Fairies

The Pet Fairies

The Fun Day Fairies

The Petal Fairies

The Dance Fairies

Read them all!

SCHOLASTIC

www.scholastic.com
www.rainbowmagiconline.com

HiT entertainment

CHOLASTIC and associated
gos are trademarks and/or
egistered trademarks of Scholastic Inc.
2009 Rainbow Magic Limited.
T and the HIT Entertainment logo are
ademarks of HIT Entertainment Limited.

RMFAIRY

SPECIAL EDITION

Three Books in One!
More Rainbow Magic Fun!

www.scholastic.com
www.rainbowmagiconline.com

HIT and the HIT Entertainment logo are
trademarks of HIT Entertainment Limited.
© 2009 Rainbow Magic Limited.
SCHOLASTIC and associated logos are trademarks
and/or registered trademarks of Scholastic Inc.

HiT entertainment

RMSPECIAL2